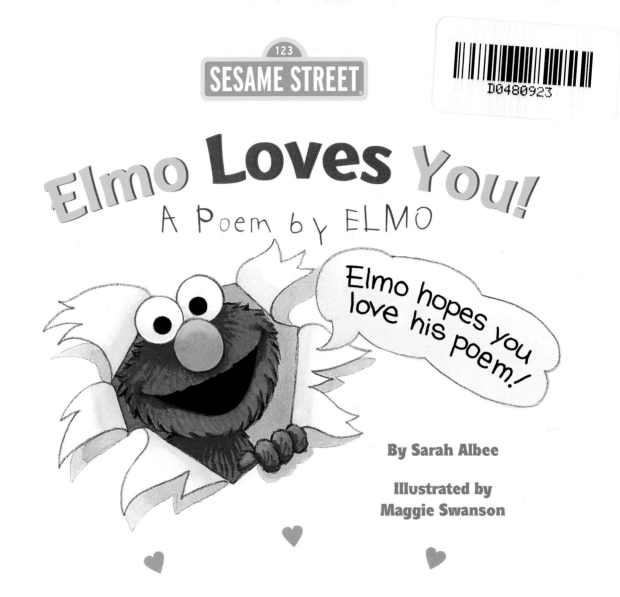

Elmo Loves You!
A Poem by ELMO

Elmo hopes you love his poem!

By Sarah Albee

Illustrated by
Maggie Swanson

Dalmatian Press, LLC, 2008. All rights reserved.
Published by Dalmatian Press, LLC, 2008. 1-866-418-2572 The DALMATIAN PRESS name and logo are trademarks of Dalmatian Press, LLC, Franklin, Tennessee 37067. No part of this book may be reproduced or copied in any form without written permission from the copyright owner.

Printed in the U.S.A.

11 12 13 B&M 37458 10 9 8 7 6 5 4
17198 Sesame Street 8x8 Storybook: Elmo Loves You!

Aa Bb Cc Dd Ee

Everyone loves something.
Babies love noise.
Birds love singing.

Kids love toys.

Bert loves pigeons,
and pigeons love to coo.
Can you guess who Elmo loves?
Elmo loves *you!*

Piggies love to roll in mud.

Penguins love the snow.

Farmers love to wake up early.
Roosters love to crow.

Zoe loves the library. Grover loves it, too.
Elmo whispers quietly, "Elmo loves *you!*"

The Count loves counting things.

Ernie loves to drum.

Monsters love to exercise.

Kids love bubble gum.

Natasha and her daddy love playing peekaboo.
But—*psssst!*—before you turn the page...
Elmo loves *you!*

Everyone loves something.
Elmo told you this was true.
And now you know who Elmo loves:
Elmo loves *you!*

Before Elmo ends his poem,
Elmo wants to ask you this:
Will you be Elmo's valentine?
Can Elmo have a kiss?

What are some things that you love?